Places And Spaces

Places And Spaces

A Book of Poems

CONNIE SWAILS THIBODEAU

To order additional copies of this book, contact:
2301 E Mesquite Ave Unit 3, Las Vegas NV 89101
info@stevenspress
(702)   508-6837
|(702)   508-6824
(702)   508-6835

Contents

OF NATURE BORN

ON GROWING OLD

BLESSINGS OF FAMILY

A FEW MORE POEMS

Introduction

The following collection of poems was written over thirty-year period. They come from my heart and reflect my thoughts, fears, feeling, joys, loves and questions about my life and my relationships especially the one with God. It is my prayer that the poems entertain you, bring you a sense of peace, make you laugh and some may bring a tear or two. But most of all I hope they touch your heart and your spirit and inspire you to greater things.

I have shamelessly used true stories from my family as inspiration. Nature has always been a valuable part of my life and much inspiration has come from my back yard with its many trees, simple wildlife and wonderful colors. The family's pets have also added some color of their own. My career as a nurse, counselor and teacher have added a depth of inspiration that is very close to my heart.

I appreciate the encouragement I have received from friends who have supported my efforts to compile and publish this collection of poems. Thanks to Kay Jones, Susan Toole, Hope Threadgill, my husband, Pete Thibodeau, my son, Matthew Thibodeau, my daughter, Heather Brownlee and others I've had the courage to share the poems with you.

OF SPIRIT BORN

When I Wander

There's a silence in the stillness
That only the soul can know.
It speaks a special language
To us mortals here below.
We seek to know the power
Of God's wondrous displays
When all along, it's captured
In the music that He plays.
The voices of the birds and wind
Stir the soul to seek.
Beauty in each passing hour
And glory in His speech.
Speak to me of the vast unknown
Of faith and love and power.
Let me hear the song of love
As I pass this precious hour.
Let faith replace the fear
And forever hold me near.
Lord of all that I survey
Hear me truly when I pray.

What Is Real?

When you ask what life is for
Or think to wish upon a star.
How would you spend your precious time?
Alone or with a cherished lover?
Which can better serve your need
Private thoughts or the touch of another?
Will prayer ease the questioning soul?
Will words sooth the pain you feel?
You ask the question all men ask,
What my Lord is truly real?

Quiet of the Mind

In the quiet of the mind,
There is a vision
That to my eyes is blind.
It is not a place
That says you're here,
But a peace that lets me care.
I lay aside my doubts and fears.
The light of God enfolds my being.
Love surrounds my senses reeling.
Devine presence heals my mind.
With this love I can't be blind.

Divine Proof

When in silence you do seek
A quiet time or one to speak
When you ask what life is for
Or think to wish upon a star.
Will prayer ease the questioning soul?
Will words sooth the pain you feel?
With your heart bursting with need
You venture out to discover truth
To discover God's divine proof.

A Child of God

Into this life I came
A child of God and of man
Lessons to learn with many rules
Of the spiritual and of the land.
Years of structure shaped my mind
And led to choices of the healing kind.
The lesson that I've yet to learn
Is how to love and live or is it mine to earn?

Life

Life is but a shell that holds us for a while
To teach some lesson on this journey's last mile.
We are not the cold blue skin on a painted face.
We are more than hostile people sharing the same dark space.
We are an enduring light
That heals the darkest night.
God has many mansions kept for those who come
To know the way that they must go and where they really come from.
Perhaps it was death when we were born to learn how not to sin.
And when we die from this life, we begin in heaven again.
To love and forgive seems the greatest task.
To seek forgiveness from those we love.
And forgive without being asked.
Teach me, Lord, to do
Thy will in all my life to live
And give me patience in my walk and courage to forgive.

Energies Reborn

I close my eyes so I can see
With my mind and ears.
Water bathes from head to toe
And draws me ever near
The gentle sounds give needed balance
To a breezy morn.
I clear my mind and relax
My energies reborn.

I Trust

I trust the voice I do not hear
With the body's ears.
Those soft and gentle words of praise
Have comforted me for years
Of growth and age and time.
I kept the promise firm,
I know my journey's end
I'm here to grow and learn.

He Sent His Son

I can't see the wind that blows
Nor hear the tide that rules the sea.
I don't know how birds learn to fly
Nor the duties of a bee.
I don't know why the earth spins
Or mountains rise to the sky.
I don't know why trees grow.
I don't know why I cry.
But I know that my God
Loves me as his own.
He sent His son to show the way
And with him I know I belong.

I Search for the Truth

I search for truth
Not knowing what I'll find.
A bit of proof
I seek—sometimes I am blind.
In what words or deeds or things
Will the answers be found?
What must I know of life and love and pain?
To what must I be bound?
Is the truth in a face
Or in a smile or tear?
Is it found in a special place?
Is it far or near?
Is the truth in another's mind?
Or is it in my own?
I search for answers I can't find.
Lord where do I belong?
I know God's light resides in me
He will guide me to be free
And teach me of his eternal peace.

I Stand

I stand transfixed with this blank gaze
Upon some ancient distant rage.
What is the scene before mind's eye?
A flicker of past lives gone by.
This image I see, where emptiness lies
Is it the story of how one dies?
Separate, alone without a well wish,
Is this a truth or a much-rehearsed pitch?
Alone in a body, but not in the mind.
At one with God, no longer blind.

Who Will Try?

Deep within I breathe a sigh,
Who will try?
Who will try?
We live and linger, and we die.
Who knows why?
Who knows why?
We work and toil and sometimes play?
Shall I stay?
Shall I stay?
Who will find reward and who will pay?
Will you pray?
Will you pray?
What brings meaning to this life?
Is it strife?
Is it strife?
Who brings joy and peace, and skill?
My Father will.
My Father will,
Faith will stay me to the end.
With God I win.
With God I win.

Moments in Time

Spaces of time
Trickling on and on
Building one after the other
Weary of life and pain and gain
Moments Too few
To many
To confusing
Too little time
Are moments time?
Moments
Less of them now
Or is that an illusion
Spaces—empty spaces
Meaning --is it loss in time
Time —an illusion to confuse the Soul
Moments—life's only reality

Legacy

It is easy to get lost
To measure life and the cost.
To think the path is straight and right
And find in remorse, perpetual night.
To know that fear has been the guide
From ageless times,
It repeats in stride.
Life gives life and lives to learn
Mostly in despair the gain is earned.
Oh, but the cost
For what is lost?

Moments Of Fear

Darkness and blackness all around
I did not feel us hit the ground.
I left the scene in fear I guess
Had I let go of this earthly quest
Of life in the bodily plane
To never see loved one's faces again.
For a brief instant in time, I was lost
But was given a second chance to pay the cost.
Where does life go in moments of fear?
Did He hold me near?
Did He show me what to do?
Did He tell me how to be true?
I know my life was in His hands
For me and my family, death was not His plan.
(Written after auto accident, 1990)

 I Am

When I tell who I am
I fear what you will do
For I am somehow different
But to me, I must be true.
I cannot follow another's path
For God made mine for me.
I must do what I think right
For I must learn to be free
From the bonds of guilt and sin
I seek to lose the ties.
That bind me to this earthy strife
And all its pain and lies.
Jesus taught us words and ways.
In His death He said he paid
For our debts both large and small.

A call he sends our way—
Come and walk and be with me
For my child I Am with thee
Though love we will be free.

Fear's Grasp

Where does peace go, in the night
When fear rides and brings in fright?
Why does it fill me with such dread?
Why the worse, why do I feel bled?
What awakes me, from sweet sleep?
To fret and wonder, without thoughts deep?
Why do I give fear such a great space?
Why can't I keep it locked in place?
Why do I listen to fearful lies?
Why can't I cut these wicked ties?
Is fear the teacher on this day?
Let it go? Let it stay?
What oh fear do you want of me?
Will you never let me be free?

I Like Words

I like words with rhythm
I like words that rhyme.
I mostly like simple words,
That say something of my time.
Words that tingle down the spine,
Words that whisper of love divine.
Words that start the foot to tap,
Words that even come out in rap.
Words that urge the "bod" to move.
Words that say get in the groove.
Words that bring the eyes to tears.
Words that soothe the hurts and fears.
Words in song of gentle praise.
Words in dance that speak of grace.
I like words that soothe the soul
And those of love that never grow old.
Give me words that say I care.
Give me words in humble prayer.

People Adorned

People adorned
Transfixed or moving
Of radiance born
Enlightened and living
Enhance our lives
With love and purity
As we transgress lies
And live with certainty
That each is blessed
In his own special way
As we renew our quest
And to God pray
That His blessing will reach
To our depths and longings
To restore faith and teach
With care and belonging.

Inner Guide

Within the winter of my feeling
Grows knowing my being.
A faint yet gentle voice,
Guides me and yet gives a choice.
A living, caring inner guide.
To trust, to lead and to provide
The self-same spirit leads all men
If they would listen and believe in Him.
He's been here since time began.
It is He who rules this land.
To Him I give a heartfelt prayer.
Thank you, Lord, for being here.

Unbounded

Bound to the earth.
Chained to gravity's spell.
Never to soar
Above the clouds
And be free and float.
Or ride the wind stream.
Dreams carry me to different places.
My Spirit.
I am free then.
Unbounded. Unchained.
Moving with the speed of light.
My heart's in flight.

Inner Spaces

Journeys take us many places.
Those of the mind to inner spaces.
We want to go where we haven't been
To see wonders of now and of then,
We want to know, to understand, to learn.
We want to know that we can earn
A life of happiness, joy and love.
We want to know there's a God above.
.When the journey comes to an end.
And we look back over where we've been
We want to say "l did it well".
I'd done enough to stay out of hell.
We want others to remember our name.
Fondly, but never in vain.
We want to know that we are loved
And remembered by God above.
No matter where the road bends
We'll find ourselves at the end.

Poetic Taste

I do not have the talent to write a poetic song.

Proper words in meter and verse don't say where I belong.

The words that flow from my pen speak of pain and doubt.

Without much thought to proper phrases. dashes, and dots.

I'm not sure from where the words come,

Only that they're given to the cadence of the dawn,

Like leaves slowly drifting from its' mother's branch.

My thoughts deliver messages, and my head goes through this dance.

I ask not from where it comes this magic in my pen.

I know that I am blessed, and these words are my friends.

A Few More Words on Words

A thought arose within my mind
A picture then I see,
I struggle to make of it some sense
And behold a word I find.
The universe and all that's in it
Has no meaning at all.
Unless we agree on what it's to be called
And that gives the thing a name—a place to fit.
Words can explain
Words can confuse
Words can hurt
And they can amuse
Words can enlighten
Words can destroy
Words can attack
And can bring some joy
Words can touch the heart
Words can lead to hate
Words can stir much discord
And lead one to forsake
Words can be patient
Words can be kind
Words can be loving
And they can be divine.
Never underestimate the power of the word.
And say it so it can be heard.

If I...

If I were a preacher,
I'd shout of his glory.
If I were a teacher,
I'd spread His great story.
If I were a doctor,
I'd know of healing.
If I were a singer,
I'd rhyme verse with feeling.
But I am a dreamer, With
the faith of a believer.
I seek to fulfill my task,
And stay on God's trusted path.

I Dreamt

I dreamt last night my Father called
And I was not prepared to go.
I asked Him if my task was done,
And He bent His head real low.
You've been given many talents child
And earthly treasures that please.
A family to care for and to love
And a gift to work with disease.
You've wasted time on guilt and worry.
And trying to keep up with others.
How would I change things if given a second chance?
Spending more time with sisters and brothers
And not giving chores a second glance.
I'd worry less.
I'd stop the stress.
That day-to-day existence brings.
I'd enjoy each day like it was spring.
I'd play more.
I'd care more.
I'd love more.
I'd give more.
I'd forgive
And truly live.

A Candle Lite

If life were like a candle lite,
That God so set to start,
To glow and warm our little world
Until we did depart.
Those who came within our glow,
Would share our space and time.
A little of our light would go with them.
A little of their light would stay with us
And, oh, how we'd shine.
Just look within your heart and see
That light shines within you and me.

Within the Center

Within the center of my feeling,
Grows a knowing of my being.
A faint yet strong and gentle voice
Guides me and yet gives a choice.
A loving, caring inner guide
To trust, to lead, and to provide.
The self-same spirit leads all men
If they would listen and believe in Him.
He's been here since time began.
It is He who rules this great land.
To Him I give a heartfelt prayer
Thank you, Lord, for being near.

If Life

If life were just a pleasant dream
And swiftly flowed from scene to scene
And magically events appear
To carry us from here to there.
If flowers went from bud to bloom
And nighttime looked like Sunday noon.
If butterflies flocked through the skies
And people never had to die.
Would I change the way I see?
Would I think me, just as free?
Would I like the way I am?
Would I know the purpose of man?

My Guardian Angel

A spark, a flicker in the dark
A warmth so lovingly touched my heart.
Did I see her misty form?
Or a fantasy, of mind born?
Who is this presence who watches over me?
Is it an angel? Can it truly be?
Not of flesh, this heavenly haunt,
Guards my life, from dusk to dawn.
She's here when I need her.
And here when I don't.

Earth Bound

A little time we have to hold
Onto our treasured dreams.
We work and scheme to make them real
And play some in between.
Life the journey begins at birth
And later returns us to the earth.
We the soul continue to be.

God calls us to be free
Of the confines of the body
We no longer wear.

Radiant light is who we are
And all is calm and clear.
I am part of God's great tree
A leaf upon the wind
To journey into new life
New duties now to tend.

To Do's

To love without fear
To give out of care
To leave without regret
To be without debt
To change and to grow
To seek high and low
To learn and to sow
To prosper and to know
To forgive
And live.

Why Me Lord?

We ask of our Father, "Why me Lord?"
Why this hurt, this pain and discord?
We look for answers we can't find.
We look for guidance from power sublime.

When the world is dark
And no light seems to shine
We struggle until we turn within
And find the Lord divine.

Meaningful Dreaming

The peace of this place gives me hope
Of better days to come.
I forget the turbulence
I've come from.
Sounds of water and endless spaces
Sounds of silence and distant places
Chirping crickets and singing birds
Churning water and kinder words.
Colors of green before my eyes
Cloud cover in distance skies.
Falling water to sooth my senses
Autumn coolness to lower defenses
Let this day be filled with joy.
Let us build and not destroy.
Let us fill each other's need.
Bless us dear Lord please.

A Tiny Drop

If truth can be found
In the words I say.
Then miracles abound,
In the verse I pray.
The heart can find the answer
To each troubling thought.
It can tell of danger
It knows what is taught.
If God can be compared
To a vast divine sea,
What grandeur He had shared
With the tiny drop called me.

OF NATURE BORN

A Walk in The Woods

I took a walk through a dark wood
And in a clearing silently stood.
The stillness captured and held me bound
To a moment without time or sound.
Loveliness and grace then filled my mind.
To all but beauty, I was blind.
A sense of peace flowed through me then,
All of nature knew me as friend.
I learned of strength and power from a tree.
A butterfly taught me how to be free.
From a berry-bush I learned of sharing.
From a deer I learned of caring.
From a flower I learned of beauty.
From the bee I learned of duty.
The wind whispered lazily through the trees,
With a song of praise on the breeze
I sought to sit, and rest and ponder,
From this place, I had no need to wander.
Visions appeared before my eyes,
For a moment there were no lies.
I knew God in all living things
And saw the goodness this earth brings.
I saw the cycle of growth in each season,
The spark that is life, I was privileged to see.
And found all things to be a part of me.
All too soon the silence broke And
from this peace, a word He spoke
And all of nature began to sing.
And praise God's Holy name.

River

When I was young much younger than today.
A place compelled me to linger and stay.
It held a special magic in its
Curvy, winding ways,
As the deep dark waters traveled
Towards the ocean's waves.
Black as the night, it lured me in
And teased me as nothing ever will again.
Memories don't just go away
They find a heart place, and forever stay.

Dirt Roads

An old dirt road leads me back
To the way things used to be.
Simple are the illusions
That my mind lets me see-
Sandy fields, moss on trees, overgrown patches
Amber straw, scraggly pines, and drainage ditches.
Mirrored Cyprus on calm dark water,
Dotted white fields where cotton was harvested.
Ancient tractors, clapboard houses and tobacco barns
Cattails in boggy swamps
In a time of simple wants.

Creation

The things that mean the most to me
Are as changeless as the sea.
I love the crash of morning waves
And the feel of tidal sprays.
By what hands are waves brought forth
To lap the sands in timeless dance.
Does the sea know its' worth?

What gave it birth?

Who tells the tides to come and go?
Who told the moon how to glow?
Who told the sky to be blue and vast?
Who told the stars to come and last?
Who made the clouds on a rainy day?
Who placed the sun in the sky to stay?
Who told the earth to turn and turn?
Who told the sun to forever burn,
Who put the trees in the forest and hills?
Who made the flowers with their colors and frills?
Who told the birds to sing out loud?
Who created fluffy white clouds?
What started this earthly journey of man?
Who guides him with unseen hands?
Creation is not a thing of chance
It's God's eternal dance.

Renewing Grace

God's renewing grace
Brings spring to this place.
The stir of gentle breeze
That close winter freeze
Birds singing melodies
Bees humming rhapsodies
Colors aglow on daffodils
Irises add their beautiful frills
Light red, then new green growth
Signal life's renewing birth.

Cycles of Life

Day follows night as summer follows spring
Ssummer's warmth to grow things
Autumn's colors adorn our lives
Then winter sneaks in and resides,
In our hearts and minds.
We think of life divine.
Winter will lose it grip
When spring rains abound.
Another cycle of life as buds
Break the ground.

Backyard Jungle

In our backyard jungle, amid the clutter and weeds
Stalks mighty hunters hidden in scrubs and trees.
The yellow-breasted sparrow scans the gutters edge
It swoops to snare a moth on a window's ledge.
The sparrow too is hunted; it would be a tasty catch
It knows not of the dangers from the neighbor's furry cat.
Our mighty hunter Remo is poised for the kill
But the closest he gets to the bird, is the inside windowsill.

Moon

The crescent glow of evening moon
Hazy clouds hanging on ends.
Rain in the air the old ones would say
Shadows of night obscuring the day.
Blessings gather round in circles
Radiating out in many purples
And in time touch the earth.
Light less brilliant than the day
A reflection of the brighter light rays.
But present and beautiful in its half-light to fall
Making midnight like morning' s call
So terribly quiet and still,
The hush before the day's storm
Of rush and hast is born.
It hangs low in the sky
You can see it if you try.
What elegance, what delight
To see the moon on this night.

Flower or Weed

What's the difference between
A flower and a weed?
One depends on the care of man,
The other the wind and the seed.
One is grown on special plots.
The other is sown on vacant spots.
Which is prettier to the senses?
The one in the vase or the one on the fences?

What lovelier sight to behold,
Than in a garden with colors bold?
Where beauty reaches to enfold.
And man's efforts are lovingly told.
But lovely is the vacant lot
Where morning glories
Cover every spot.
Or the unmowed lawn
Where dandelions grow
And proclaim beauty
With their bright yellow glow.
A special place in cycles of time
For weeds tease the senses
And please the mind.

Light

We can see the sun and feels its rays.
We know of its' presence in natures grand displays.
It lights our days and warms our nights.
It signals good and leads to right.
What wonderous gifts it brings
From budding flowers to bubbling springs,
It brings us love and laughter too.
It brings us the light and we renew.

If A Tree

If a tree could get up and move...
Where would it go?
Would it move quick?
Or would it move slow?
Would it find a quiet place?
Beside a lovely brook?
Or would it favor a nosier life
Inside a city nook?
Would it grow straight and tall,
In a rural meadow
Or cramped and wild in a city ghetto?
If a tree had one wish
What could that wish be?
Would it choose to be like
You and me?
Lonely, afraid and too tired to move,
Or happy contented with the ability to choose,
Or bitter and angry, believing no one cares,
Or nurturing, forgiving with someone to share?
What would it say of my life?
Would it give words of advice?
Learn to bend and not to break.
Learn to love and never hate.
Learn to give and be forgiven.
Learn to forgive and not be driven.
Trees grow where they planted.
Thank you, Lord, for all you've granted.

Live Plants

In amongst the weeds and grass
Live spiders, crickets and bug,
They're OK out there,
But not in the living room rug

Other night creatures grace our home and yard,
From silvery, blue lizards
To our happy canine guard.

There is one more thing that troubles me
As fall colors nature adorns,
When I bring my plants inside
Will creatures be reborn?
The plants thick branches and roots
May conceal some hide away,
Spiders. lizards and snakes—
Not welcome is what I'll say

The Wind Song

The wind whistles through the trees
And branches swing in coming freeze.
The icy wind blows louder still
As the shrill song echoes through the hills.
It plays with leaves and scatters then about
As it howls distant warnings out.
"Face me, face me if you will
My icy fingers they can kill."
But the song will cease to be
As spring returns to set earth free?
A gentler song upon the land
The wind is calmed by the hand.
That guides all life to unfold
And gives such grandeur to behold.

Life Renewing

Winter gray gives way to light
And warms the air as birds take flight
Naked limbs await the spring

As crows give out a resounding ring.
Browns and grays highlight the earth
And lets us know of her worth.
I await spring's song of love

And remember God's gifts from above,
Warmth of the sun: lilies in bloom.
Sounds of the water to erase the gloom.
Life renewing change the season.

Away with winter for so many reasons.

Transition

I like falls bright clear days.
The colors with many hues and shades
Of purple, orange, yellow and red
And browns the shade of the dead.
Warm, sunny autumn skies.
Cool nights with no fireflies.
To stroll by a gentle brook
To listen to the splash and look.
As nature danced to time's decay
To know of age and yet to stay,
And watch as time passes by
And know that I cannot die.

Contrasts

Winds from the north bring a chill to the air
Listen a while and hear
The call of winter and quiet delight,
Curled in warmth with a good book
Looking forward to cozy sleep tonight.

Evening Falls

Night sounds entice the listening ear
As the dark curtain falls ever near.
Shadows deepen in dark decent
As the suns fading rays are quietly spent.

The cricket sings to snare a moth
And signals that the day is lost,
The bullfrog declares -it's getting late
Come in, come in beckons the light,
And leave this eerie night.
(June 1991)

Oh, Misty Morn

Oh, misty morn uninviting and cold,
Some cry and scorn; others venture out bold.
What secrets lie hidden in winter's gray hue?
What dream is forbidden away from view?
Trees laid bare the season of change
Branches reach out in hopes of gain.
Flowers now gone that blossomed in spring.
Seeds lay dormant and await May's rain.
Autumn colors fade to shades of brown.
Fallen leaves blanket now bare ground.
All life is not stopped by winter's cold hand
For birds still sing and take a firm stand.
Water still churns in an endless stream
As morning light breaks the mist in warming sun beams,
Crows play tag in near-by trees
Squirrels scamper amongst a blanket of leaves
My mind is quieted in this place.
I am richly blessed.
Thanks, Father, for giving your best.

Where Is the Flower?

Where is the flower that I once knew?
Along this trodden path?
Did it die and start anew
A different sort of task?
It did grace this winding road
With its tender glow.
By what power, by whose hand
Did its' life flow?
Could it not linger here and brighten up my day?
Lord above answer me,
Why can't beauty stay?

Seasons

Seasons come and seasons go.
Sometimes in a fury.
Sometimes very slow.
One barely leaves, before the other awakens.
Winters here and life is taken.
Spring will break in plants and trees,
Birds, butterflies and humming bees,
Spring will slip into summer's hot days.
Things grow in the sun's hot rays.
Warm nights; a million-star lights
Fireflies take flight, the moons full bright.
Apples are red and new life wings.
We know before long what shorter days bring.
The chill in the air stirs the crimson and gold
Leaves in a flurry let go of their hold.
You know before long what the winds will bring.
Storms of winter, less birds to sing.
Winter's drab blankets the land.
All things sleep, by God's hand.
Browns now adorn forest and field
Do you wonder if it's all real?
Ice and snow will linger a while
And then depart like a playful child.
Again, the cycle anew begins
And we're reassured that life doesn't end.

Nightfall

Night in infancy grew
A sliver of moon peaked above the horizon.
As trees bare boned in winter's death,
Framed against the decline
Of blue, to gray to purple sky.
Day lingered no more And
left the darkening earth.
Night shadows emerged from hiding.
Definition faded into the obscure
Less form, objects coalesce,
Molding into creatures
Of the worrisome sort.
Lights flicker on then off,
Then on to stay.
To greet the night
And give pretense of day.

If Trees Had Memories

If trees had memories and thought of things to come
Would they wonder if tomorrow would bring the glorious sun?
Would they think of bygone days?
Where their life was uncertain and fragile
And hope that things will stay
The way they are without a trifle?
Would they look around and see
Illness, old age and poverty?
Would they see what man's machines can do?
Would they live in uncertainty and become blue?
Would they plot and think to prolong their life?
Or would they settle for a world of painful strife?
Would they think of owning the ground their roots invade?
Or would they just be thankful for the years they've stayed?
But trees are not like you and me.

God gave us a mind and a plan you see,
Trees exists for us to tend,
To enjoy and mend.

But there's much to learn from a wise old oak,
What a story a tree could tell if ever it spoke.
A thing of beauty is the tree.
And in its own way it is free.

Dusk

Fireflies light the dusky sky
As daytime embers slowly die.
Each one a beacon in the night
Off and on with much delight,
They climb into the cool night air,
As if to tempt and try to snare a mate,
To entice life's perpetual dream
And assure nature's yearly theme.
The joys of an early summer's night
Can stir the senses by early moon light.

I find Comfort

I find comfort in—
The power of healing water
The beauty of early fall
The trees becoming nude
The ripples in a muddy pond
The dance of a butterfly
The contour of a garden wall
The warmth of a new blue sky
The gentleness in swaying trees
The touch of falls beginning breeze
The freshness of the morning dew
Summer days now down to a few.
The fragrance of an unnamed flower
The majesty of an oak tree tower
The awesomeness of a bird's wing
The smell of dampness in the air
From yesterday's rain
Couples walking in pairs
The birds continue to sing
Blessings abound in all I see
And in all I touch and feel.
Teach me Lord to train my mind
That this is what is real.
Thank you for the cycles of life
With changes everywhere
Eternal seasons come and go
But life is always here.

Edisto

I like to sit beside the sea
Behold work of His majesty.
Endlessly washing to the shore.
Waves crash with familiar roar.
The sun, the sound, the breezy air
Salty foam adorns the beach.
Shells—a life now spent.
Witnessing God just out of reach.
The sounds of the sea, do call to me
To come, to experience to be free.
Warm sand beneath my feet
What a joy to be at the beach.

New Day

Distant skies, with distant callings.
Different people, different longings.
Troubled minds and emotions
Unloved lacking devotion.
Peaceful dreams in quiet places
Seeking out some mystical meaning.
Amidst the lying and scheming.,
Needing love and belonging.
Awaken now, a new day is dawning.

Beaty of Spring

There is much beauty in the spring.
In colors, growth and the way birds sing.
Harmony is called to mind
To winter's wrath we are now blind.
Cycles of life within the seasons.
Joyous wonders forever pleasing
Spring rains and gentle showers.
Longer days more sunlight hours.
Gardeners tending freshly plowed ground.
Gone are fields of countless browns.
Shades of green, blanket the fields.
As God's mysteries slowly reveal.
One more spring to delight the senses
In God's world no borders or fences.

Journey of the Mind

Early autumn and a feel to the air
A release, a belief and a care.
Life's endless cycles of death and birth
Is it a blessing or a curse?
Days are shorter: stillness fills my heart.
I know in spring there'll be a new start.
Days and months and even years
In numbers yet untold.
Earth's journey through time is foretold.
Will life continue as before?
For the travelers who journey on earth.
Is it time for a new birth?
The second coming is it of the heart?
Have we already begun our part?
Are lines drawn on the sands of time?
To end this journey of the mind.

Weeds

I am a special flower
Sometimes called a weed.
I grow in many places
Sometimes not where I am wanted.
Birds and bees like my many hues
And visit when I display.
My color, my beauty and face the sun.
I scatter my seeds to the wind
To travel and start life anew.
And repeat the endless cycle
Of life, death and decay
My life is short, my beauty profound,
I take from the earth
And give back beauty and substance
To other entities in my life
In my death I replenish the soil and give again.

Reflections of Life

The path I chose was old and worn
Others chosen were newly born.
Sun streaks bathed the forest floor
To highlight nature's abundance galore.
I chanced upon a sheltered place
Where ferns grew and found their space
I discovered much to delight the senses
And found no need for walls and fences.
Trees and humming bees
Faded blossoms and cackling crows
Playing squirrels and crocking toads
Katydids and monkey grass
Steamy forest and windy paths
Turtle posed over water's edge
Crawly things on a rocky ledge
Wildflowers sown by the wind
Something new at each new bend.
Fish barely visible in murky depths.
What secrets in these waters are kept?
Couples in pairs—uneasy starts,
Journey awhile and part.
Camellias hung with pine needle icicles
Life repeating in endless cycles.
Ducks afloat in varying colors
A walk in the woods for many others.
Reflections of life in still waters
Visions of hope in natures' quarters.
Life abundant surrounds this place
Filling a need -an empty space.
Oh, what a blessing a gentle breeze
On this day of leisure and ease.

Yellow Dandelions

All along the roadways in my lengthy drive
Carpeted yellow Dandelions
And Daisies brighten my ride.
Lovely are the flowers of spring
Ushered in with gentle rain.
Dogwoods, Azaleas and Daylilies too,
Welcome the season bright and new.
Songs of birds in nesting mode
Greet me on this winding road
All is spring, wherever I see,
Lord thank you and please bless
All others and me.

The Mocking Bird

The mockingbird lights up the morn
With its song of joy.
Taking from his feathered friends
Repeats, their songs to all.
So, like this versatile bird
To pick up another's song
And announce to all who hear
Morning has been born.
What joy it brings to my heart
To hear his many tunes,
Reminding me that I to
Will flower and bloom.

This Day

At water's edge I stop and listen
To an ancient sound both loud and whispered.
Echoes of a distant past
When life was all brand new and made to last,
When concerns and problems
Of men were few,
And man' purpose was to learn and renew.
Did He know I would ponder?
And through this garden wander?
Did He know I'd ask?
"How long will it last?"
Water from cascading falls.
Plants galore on rocky walls.
Trees stretching branches high
Birds in flight against the sky.
This beauty fills all my senses
Down come a few more fences.
As I listen and recall
He did make it all.

ON GROWING OLD

Age

Age is a funny word,
That has much to say.
What age am I?
What age is now?
What age is old?
What age says how?
What age says why?
In what age must I die?

Is age a truth?
Is age a game?
Is age proof?
Is age the same,
For each soul who travels here?
When will we know
When we are near?
To the promise of eternal life?
When will we know the price?
That all men pay for living here?
What will calm my questioning mind?
To truths let me not be blind.

Middles

It's very tempting when I start a new book,
To turn to the end and chance a look.
To see how time and distance and choices
Have brought about blessings, as well as losses.
To skip the part about pain and fears,
And see what was learned through the years.
Beginnings and endings without many middles,
Mean excitement and regrets without solving the riddles.
Middles are part of the journey we take

Where we trust and we learn from the mistakes.
Goodbyes are many on this path of life.
Some are bought with pain and strife.
Others are part of the "Passages" we make.
Still others the result of the chances we take.
To start a new book and continue to grow,
Let the lessons slowly flow.

Summer's Dream

I've often wondered if others in middle age
Wished they could replay their life like on a stage.
Select a character off the screen,
Go through each movement of the scene.
See oneself in passionate embrace
Remembering in youth
It would have been a disgrace.
To follow desires, passions and heart.
And lct youthful zeal ignite the spark.

Middle Age

To have lived half your life
You've learned of joy and love and pain.
Much you know of trouble and strife
And you've even managed to see some gain.
Did dreams and plans of childhood fail
Or did promises made in youth
Put a lock on a self-made jail?
Will it keep you from discovering the truth?
If I could go back and live life again
Would the same mistakes be made?
If knowledge of half-a-life began
When I was twenty and not yet paid
The debt of my choices both right and wrong
And knew with certainty where I belonged.
Would I use the knowledge gained through time?
To help others or would I be blind?
Would I seek only the power of money and success
Or would I seek peace and thy bliss?
Oh, Lord would it matter if I could go back
Would I still see my poverty, and want and lack?
Or would I view the world with different eyes
Of wisdom and know my own lies?
The future of age somehow looks brighter
To be older, slower, and wiser.
It's enough to ask for in the middle years
To see the beauty in my tears.
Does each generation look back with wonder?
And long for the joys of a remembered summer.

Self

I am but a wanderer in the vast expanse of man.
I see no boundaries or borders on God's eternal land.
The fleshy body that man cherishes so,
Is but a simple house for our
Soul to seed and grow.
The body can do but little, without the powerful mind.
But to this simple truth many are still blind,
To the self of which we most often speak.
Look within to the other Self
For it is where you'll find true help.
Learn the place of silent prayer.
Receive His light through gentle care.
Explore the depths of truth and faith.
Find your purpose in an inner space.
Cherish the peace that dwells within.
It is then you'll understand,
To life there is no end.

Persistence

I feel like an alien in a dark land
Where dreams are made and carved by hand.
Where each fragment of truth is tendered with care.
But few give witness only those most dear.
Many are taught to enter the fold
And learn how to let the plan unfold.
Few survive the vigorous task,
Only a few can truly last.
Changes tugged from depths untold
Bring forth fears yet to unfold.
Can I endure the terminal growth?
Can I be strong for us both?
Can we achieve this path?
Oh Lord do make it last.
Let me be open to all new things.
And know the love peace brings.
I'll do my best, then and now.
Help me Lord to make it somehow.

Comes The Night

Comes the night in purples and grays
Leaves the sun I murky haze.
Shadows now where light did reign.
Darkness creeps, no forms remain.
Sleep comes in time. Rest sublime.
Dreams so soft and sweet
Or of fear and deceit.
Tossing, turning afraid now to sleep.
What is the meaning that one seeks?
Night gives way to orange-red glow.
What beauty will day bestow?
The answer is within me.
It's all around to see.

In My Youth

Nothing is as clear as in my youth
For then I knew what life was for.
I blaze my way through age
To come to death's door.
Is this the end?
Did I pass the test?
In heaven's splendor
Will I rest?
Tell me not the other place.
Can it be worse than this space?
Where limits impose my every turn.
My mind says move
My body can't respond
And again I lose.

A Frightened People

A frightened people we have become
Discipline of body and mind succumb.
We escape our thoughts through media events,
With politics, religion and science pretense.
Our religions do not serve us well.
They say our pleasures will take us to hell.
What will we gain in future lives?
If we talk and tell a few more lies.

Probable Realities

The likeness of me I see in thee
For we are one, you and l.
We live, we breathe, we form, we see.
Together we create what is to be.
You are you and I am me.
Separately we go our way,
But into life we go much further
And find we fit and play.
Our minds are part of a greater one
That gives us life and more.
We create each new day of life.
As we struggle to restore
The grandeur of a different world,
Not marred by doubt and shame.
A world of peace and love and beauty
Not one that's filled with pain.
We seek to find from whence we came,
To explore all possible worlds.
We want to know what makes us tick,
And who makes the stars to twirl.
We create for ourselves
The life we are to share.
We think the thought,
We act the scene.
We think of tomorrow and we dream.

Fif of Dispair

Timed obsolescence.
Linear demise.
Downward body cycle.
Return to origin.
Glory to gain.
Or hell's eternal flame.

Will I Win?

With some days joy
And some days fears,
The seeds we plant
Through passing years.
We reap rewards
And sometimes tears.
Looking backwards thru this life?
What is gained by the strife?
What did I give to those I know?
Will I be remembered as friend or foe?
As my days come to an end
Tell me Lord will I win,
A home in Thy Holy place,
Somewhere that's my special space?

Counting

Count the minutes in a day.
Count the acts within the play.
Count the trees that line the path.
Count the years as they past.
Count the choices you have made.
Count the ones for which you prayed.
Count the blossoms on a flower.
Count the blessings of this hour.
Count the friends throughout the years.
Count the battles and the tears.
Count the children at their play.
Count the reasons why you stay.
Count the droplets in a brook.
Count the chances that you took.
Count the ways your life has changed.
Count the times you've shared the shame.
Count the many ways to learn.
Count the times you've truly earned.
Count the ways you've been loved.
Count your blessings from above.
All things are equal in this hour
By God's holy, awesome power.

A New Line of Thought

My mind is confused by a new line of thought.
Wondering how this body was bought.
What thought led to aging lines?
When did I say I wanted to be blind?
By what route did I choose this pain?
Did I believe there was something to gain,
In being old and overweight?
Did I think I needed to hate?
The point of power is in the now.
My thoughts are waiting to show me how
To change beliefs of time and decay,
And find peace in me on another day.

Win or Defeat

I've asked myself all my life
Which way to go, which way is right?
It is not clear to me at all
The logic in God's merciful call.
Some he calls early in life,
Others spend counted years of pain and strife.
Some seemed blessed along their way
Yet others really don't want to stay.
Some find meaning in all they see.
Some are happy, at peace and free.
Some struggle to give life their best
Some live as if life were a test.
If goodness is measured by the struggles, we meet.
Then goodness abounds in a win or defeat.

Aged By Time

Aged by time and wrinkled skin
Led by desire to live and win.
Limited choices now unfold
Less stories now to be told.
"Retire to what" one may ask?
Just more time to complete the task.
What magic comes to later years,
From youthful moments of joys and tears?
Leave the work to others now,
Learn other "what's" and "how's".
Enjoy more leisure and time alone.
Learn new rights and new wrongs.
More time to spend with kids and such,
More time to think,
No need to rush.

Parting

When age and time, bring to an end
The sharing of life's paths.
And we look back at where we've been
Will we see plenty or lack?
Were we all that we could be?
Did we count our blessings then?
Did we think to care?
We have spent both days and nights
Seeking to give to others.
In the lessons we have shared,
Can we now live as sisters and brothers?
Truths are not so easy to find.
Thoughts get in the way.
Jobs to do and do them well
They even consume us when we pray.
Turn not with regret
When your time is done.
Your rest is earned
A new life now begun.
For God will not be undone.

On Being Old

Take my hand and talk to me,
For I have need to be with thee.
I'm not young and spry anymore
I'm old and gray and a bit of a bore
To the young folk who think life a joke
Who're unable to listen when an old one spoke.
What can I tell you of my life and time?
That will mean something when
I no longer have a mind.
There's nothing I can give you
Now to take the place of me.
But let your memories flow as
You hear me in the sea.
Perhaps I'll sing a song in the wind
Or chill you on a snowy mountain top and then
You'll see my smile on another's face
Or see me in some distant place.
Let me go to God's waiting hands
And fulfill His wondrous eternal plan.

Passing

With the passing of the years
We feel the joy, the pain and fears.
As age and time take its toll,
Bodies age and grow old.
We know the time is growing near.
What will we do when they're not here?
Alas, God calls them to His side
And we'll get by, we will survive.
This journey is as old as man
To cross over to a distant land,
A land of gentle quiet peace
A place that's within our reach.
Bless the ones we leave behind,
Give them love and joy divine.

Retiring

Past the autumn of life's time
Enter winter's cycle sublime.
Witness the freedom of life's decline.
Fewer days ahead and more behind.
What gifts await you through these years?
What joys, what hopes and what fears?
Life unfolds as never before,
As you walk though, yet another door.
With hope you leave what you have known,
And venture out, but not alone.
We have seen you through the years.
We conquered many fears and tears.
Each day we laid a brand-new stone.
Through the work we have grown.
Our paths now lead in separate ways,
We will miss you for we must stay.

Oh, Time

Oh, time—time of yesteryear.
Distant, but mindfully clear.
When simpler thoughts filled my mind.
What has changed the way I see?
What thoughts will set me free?
To youth's vigor I applaud.
Is ages' wisdom to answer the call?
In the middle, between birth and death
Halfway between one and the other.
How many years to me are left?
If time shapes who am,
Then grant me what is mine,
Not the riches of the earth,
But those of a loftier kind.
Do not punish mistakes I've made,
For it's the debt that must be paid.

On Turning Sixty

If life is worth the living as we're so often told,
Then when is life more thrilling, for the young or the old?
Youth has many virtues like motivation, energy and time,
And many plans and promises of the youthful kind.
What though is the promise of a longer life?
Besides charming children and a loving wife.
We wanted to prepare you for the coming years,
Routines don't change from years fifty-nine to sixty.
Deciding what to eat, gets a little ricky.
Geritol gets you though your day,
And prune juice sends you on your way.
But with loose dentures, it's so hard to chew.
Many days behind, but you still have a few.
The bathroom schedule is less of a bore,
After the ExLax—don't bar the door.
Added years mean less hair to comb,
And the Grecian Formula, doesn't last as long.
You'll have more time to spend on fun
But less money to buy shells for the gun.
Fishing can still occupy some time,
Even with a wandering mind.
What makes a person somehow old?
Is it fear of change as we've been told?
Be mindful of this time of your life.
Cherish well, what you've earned in strife.
May all sixty-year old's find their heart's delight.
Joyous days, much love, and truly peaceful nights.
You will go, but we will stay.
Many blessings we pray.

Growing Old

Deep furrows on her ancient face.
Distant look from some inner space
Troubled eyes
Much sorrow has seen
Weakened body
Little left of youthful gleam.
Weary now
Of stress and strife.
Little left
Of the pleasures of life.
Waiting for
Deaths sure door.
Wondering
What it's all been for.
Will Heaven be a peaceful place?
With God's promise of eternal grace?
Will the wealth of love and lasting joy,
Be there for us all to enjoy?
Or will we find to our dismay
A sad place of eternal decay?
God said we'd have a peaceful space
And I believe in his Grace.

A Puzzle

If time is spent
And space is traveled
We are doomed to come unraveled.
We wander aimless
In timeless space

And space our time
For a distant place.
If now is here
And here is now
What other reality
Will takes its bow?
To know this moment
As my own
Will it leave me all alone?

A Journey Complete

Within the blinking of the eye
One body is born and one body dies.
This cycle of life brings growth and decline.
In our youth we think we're divine
And that there is no end to time.
Some never question where they began.
In middle years we question all things
And resolve to see what tomorrow brings.
In later years of regrets, we sing
Until we know love and what it brings.
Death leaves an empty hole
That only time can heal.
And those left here,
Learn what is real.
A long-lived life, a journey complete.
A new path now; a new retreat.
God's time is not our own.
In Gods time we'll all go home.

What Is My Task?

Tell me what my task must be
On this human journey.
Will I be strong and a leader of men?
Or a follower who struggles to lend—
A hand to the needy, a gift to the poor
A word to the puzzled, a keeper of score,
A smile to a stranger or to the ill
A praise for the child with a new skill
Will I walk proudly to do my duty? Or
struggle to find a little beauty
Or will I scold, and blame and regret
And let bitterness lead to neglect.
Will I thank God for being near
And giving me the strength to bare
The pain of living life
And following his grand plan.
Lord it is madness to be in this space
But I know I'll make it by your Grace.

Nearing the End

If there is a lighter side of life
Amidst the pain and the strife.
If there is joy and happiness to be found
In life's daily ups and downs.
If success is within our reach
If we are destined here to teach
Others by our daily deeds,
And help them through their wants and needs.
If troubles remind us of who we are
Then time will tell us just how far
We must go before we reach
The beauty of God's eternal peace.
When age and time have stolen our youth
And we've discovered what we know as truth.
We cling to memories old and new
And cherish friendships that are true.
Linger on warm summer breeze
Postpone winter's chilling freeze
Let us linger here a while,
Where others know our ways and style.
Let us share our care and love,
And give thanks for blessings from above.
This family, Lord, needs your peace
Keep them within your reach.

Locked Within

Religion was the first maker of my reality,
From tiny infant and toddler steps the journey to destiny,
Of equal power to influence my mind,
The rigidity of math, of science and of time.
What magic will undo this imposing spell?
And help me escape this self-made hell?
What can change these rigid rules?
What can unlock this unyielding school?
For answers, I look, to questions not known.
What new journey is yet to be born?

What Do You See?

Mirror on my painted wall
What is it that you see?
When you look into this room
Does the image set you free?
Do you think the room too small,
Or that the colors don't match?
Do you see events and time,
Or the limitations and lack?
When I see my aged face
Staring from your depths
I wonder where the years have gone
And think of my regrets.
What do you see when you see me?

Mirror that can tell no lie
Judge me as you may.
Show me truth before I die.
I must leave this chosen place
And venture out alone.
More days behind than before
Are the best days really gone?
My path now leads another way
And my dear ones I cannot stay.

God Made

I am an old woman
Lord only knows how many days
I have left.
I am not dead yet!
The days I have
I'll do what suits me best.
I have children and grandchildren
And they have lives of their own.
I don't have many friends
And spend a lot of time alone.
I try my best to read and keep up
But my mind doesn't focus to well.
Politics are just plain crazy
And religion says we're bound for hell.
I was born on this earthly plane from a man and woman
Where these many years I've stayed
But that's not the whole story,
Because I'm also God made!

Limited by Time

Whatever life will bring tomorrow
Is written in the wind.
We cannot know what God will do
For that is up to Him.

We may find success, joy, sadness,
Passion, failure or peace
Or a combination of things
We never thought were within our reach.

Tomorrow may be another yesterday
If we choose not to learn.
Today is tomorrow we worried about
When our place had to be earned.

Yesterday is past.
It is but a memory.
Tomorrow is to come.
Today is temporary.

With each breathe
A little part is gone.
This moment is real
In it you belong.

BLESSINGS OF FAMILY

Grandmother

Of all the roads that I have walked
Of all the classes I have taught
Of all the patients I have nursed
O fall the words I put to verse
Of all the folks I have led
Of all the miles my feet have trod
Of all the duties I have done
Of all the projects I've begun
Of all the people in my care
Of all the roles I sought to play
The one I like best today
Is not that I've cared for many others
But the one as Grandmother.

Marriage Bond

God has brought us safely here
And through our love with Him we'll share.
The bounty of a married life
As we live together as man and wife.
The bond we make as we love and give,
Provides faith, and hope and a reason to live.
What is marriage for, it not to learn.
And through the troubles and trials we earn
A rightful place in the life of man,
And learn when to challenge and take a stand.
Make a friend of each other as your journey begins
For in time, relationships strain and look grim.
Trust that your heart won't steer you wrong
And you'll make up and come back to where you belong.
Be blessed with wisdom and a long life too.
To this bond forever be true.

A Promise

My beloved I bring to you the gift of all I am,
And promise that I'll share with you in every way I can.
This love I feel, I can't explain,
In words the ear can hear.
For it's my heart that doth proclaim
I'm nothing without you near.
I've waited for you like a child waits for a treasured gift.
Seeking in each passing face the spark of divine bliss.
The peace I find when you are near
Forever binds me to you dear.
I love the smile that brightens your face.
For it reflects God's Holy Grace

Forgive me if my joy consumes and threatens you away,
Know within thy beating heart I truly want you to stay.
I know of pain and the joy of living
And am not fulfilled without the giving.
In this bond of love we seek
That's not intended for the weak.
If God would grant my fondest wish
And make my dreams come true
I'd spend each moment of my life
Forever loving you.
In this marriage we've begun
A journey through life as one,
May we find each other worthy
Of this gift we give.
And keep forever this blessed trust
For all the days we live.

Tootsie

It took time through many a year
To understand my mother's fear.
That I'd grow up with little care
For life and love and others dear.
The lessons I learned from my parents then
I find myself repeating again.
I know now what it means to feel pain and doubt,
And what's really behind a child's silent pout.
I want my children to reflect something of me.
I want them to learn how to live free.
How many of the values and beliefs will kids keep?
Will they harm or protect the weak?
How do you tell a child the meaning of life?
How do you tell them with gain comes strife?
How much of yourself do you give to another?
When does a stranger become a brother?
What are the lessons we learn in our youth?
Do they even come close to the truth?
I hear my mother's voice echoed in each thought,
She already knows what time has brought.
Our parents we trust to show us the way.
And when we need them they'll tell us to stay.
Being a mother too, I've accepted the task
To teach my children something that will last.
Mom, I thank you for all you have been.
A caregiver, a listener, and a friend.
Our views on life aren't always the same
But we know our relationship is more than a name.
May friends and family surround you this Mother's Day
And God's blessings be many—for this I pray.

Daddy

In life you blessed in many ways
And told us our time is numbered to days.
What are we to learn dad from your untimely lost?
Are we also to pay the same cost?
What will we learn from your life and deeds
Or will we think only of our own needs?
What good can come of such a tragic end?
Will your passing allow other hearts to mend?
Your body is now returned to the soil
But your soul will continue on to toil,
For God is not through with you at all.
And through memories we choose to recall.

The miracle of life so graciously given.
And the chance to go for Christ has risen.
You he called his own,
And now you have found a new home.

Worth

The ebb and flow in life's moments,
When all goes well and when it doesn't
Happiness is bought with tears,
And pain brings forth the fears.
You are like no one I've known before,
When you came you closed a door.
By what magic did you capture my mind?
By what potion was I entwined?
By what power have you stirred my heart?
How did you make the fire spark?
From the beginning as if by plan,
We met, not the first time. but once again.
You and I have traveled before,
On some timeless, nameless shore.
We've pledged our life to be free.
We fulfill all God planned us to be.
Our paths were destined to cross again,
Together we play each act in the plan.
Your growth and mine are bound as one,
We work, we grow, we love, we've begun.

For Pete

May God find you worthy
Of sweet dreams each night.
May the sandman sprinkle his dust
So tonight's sleep is just right.
May blessings be abundantly yours,
For all your years to come.
May you not get loss

On any journey you've begun.
May you live surrounded by love,
Knowing you are wanted there
And may you always have someone
To provide loving, gentle care.
When the day gets long and grey
And blessings are too few,
Remember God is always near
And a few people too.

Becoming A Family

Man and woman came to be
And in marriage did pledge to thee
To forever share, honor and love
With the gifts given them from above.
Through the years as their love grew
And to each other they were true.
God saw fit to make them three
And add a name to their family tree.
With gladness and hope they wait the birth
Of a new child to bless this earth.
Comfort this family with abundant care
And bless them with every prayer.

New Baby

The magic in a baby's face
Blessing from God through Grace.
The wonder of her joy of life
A new reason to eliminate strife
Mom and Dad she says in time.
Such a beautiful joyous rhyme.
Your heart you give as not before
She has opened another door,
Times' journey now consists of three
Bonded as one, and forever free.

Childhood

Matchbox toys to play and roll.
Friends go hand in hand to stroll.
Adventures behind each bend in the road.
Ageless stories forever told.
Winding roads to know and explore,
Trees to climb, tales to store.
Childhood- the life we try to leave,
And in later years can't believe
We'd want to leave the simple pleasures
Of warm summers and nature's treasures.

My Son

My son is tall for his age.
He thinks of life as but a stage,
Where one learns and plays a role
But no tickets to this play are sold.
In this play of quest and life
He sees himself in sacrifice and strife.
No one seems to understand his yearning
As he explores new ways of learning.
A life with purpose and love
Not yet knowing it comes from above.
He plays with ideas and beliefs
And through his friends finds no relief
In the struggle to live with himself.
He'll soon discover his true Self.
To be a teenager is no easy task
Thank God the age will past.
He'll discover his manhood
With its independence and freedom.
He will feel that he has sweat blood
And never again know of boredom.
His destiny he'll share with his power and wisdom
As he plays out the role he's been so graciously given.

For Heather

She sat staring out the door
From her place on the floor.
She wanted so to go outside
Get on her bike and ride and ride.
But the rain came storming down
The water twirled round and round.
She's played with Ken and Barbie too,
In her book she drew and drew.
Flowers, a house and a bright round sun
She drew a friend to play with
And hoped to have some fun.
She thought about what she could do.
When the rain left
And the sky turned a clear blue.

Darling Daugther

How could a mother be more blessed
Than with such a child as you?
As you embark upon your life
To thyself be true.
From child to woman
I've watched you grow.
You share yourself and on others, bestow
A grace and dignity not known to all.
A sense of humor and a special call
With an air of a mystic, you travel in time
Your gentleness given to those you call mine.
I'm proud of you every day
Especially so and in everyway
On this your graduation day.

Letting Go

The bow is steadied in the archer's hand
With much skill and with intent.
An arrow made by his own heart
Is drawn—it's time here spent.
It must now find its' special mark.
Its path he must choose and discover,
The archer draws it to his face.
His eyes with awe and wonder,
The mark it makes will spell its worth.
And through time it will grow.
With tears he sends the arrow forth
And grieves to see it go.
The arrow swift from crafted care
With purpose it leaves the bow.
The archer only knows his heart
His blessings he does bestow.
A thing of purpose must fulfill
The task for which it came.
The archer sets the arrow free
Neither man will be the same.

Graduation

Such a mixture of joy and sadness
Fill my body and mind
As I see that manly frame,
So strong and yet so kind.
Today you end your life as child
And venture out as man.
You have to pave a brand new way,
In this a changing land.
The world you inherit from your folks
Is not the one you'll know.
Somehow the world is older
And with it you must grow.
It is with much love and pride
That I see you go.
It is also with much grief
For I will miss you so.
I've watched you as you've traveled,
Though the childhood years.
I've witnessed all your struggles,
Conflicts, problems and fears.
You are the promise of tomorrow
The future is now in your hand.
Learn your lessons well my son
And change the course of man.

Kenadie Grace

The magic in a baby's face
Blessing from God through Grace.
The wonders of her joy of life
Adding meaning and lots of spice.
Momma and daddy she says in time
Such a beautiful joyful rhyme.
Your heart you give as never before
She has opened another door.
Time's journey now consists of three
Bonded as one, ever now free.
Her good you've placed above your own
Your house is now a family's home.

I'm the Oldest

My child gave birth to her child today.
What wonder and what a thrill.
Life repeating itself again
By God's holy will.
Light gold highlights in her hair
To shape her delicate face.
Blue eyes sparkle as she dresses in lace.
She's stolen the hearts of all her kin
And those of her parents' friends.

Middle Child

Little round face
Pretty black hair
A cute little body
To hold near
Ten tiny fingers
Ten tiny toes
A one-sided dimple
A perfectly formed nose
A good healthy cry
A shimmer and a sigh
Only a few days old
But my heart She's
already stole.

Youngest Child

He held her tiny head
In the palm of his hand.
Instant love held his gaze
As only your own child can.
A small perfect body
Tinier than her sisters
And a mystery to her mother.
A gentle little smile
And black straight hair
Wrinkled little knees
Thin skin most fair.
Her sisters like to hold her
And wait for her to smile.
Such a tiny precious thing
For her they'd walk a mile.

Mother's Curse

Heather said the mother's curse always rings true.
Poppy is much more like her than the other two.
She is soooo full of energy, intensity and,
With an "I want it now attitude."
She tends to rule the space and place,
With her high-pitched squeal or yell.
She generally gets what she wants.
"Give it to her", end the spell.
She'll entertain you and frustrate you.
She'll annoy you and charm you.
She will also love you and bless you with her smile.
She may crawl up in your lap cause she's just a child.

Children

Our children reap what we have sown,
Fear of discovery, fear of the unknown.
They seek the secure in thought and deed.
In their youth they deny their need.
Infinite paths before them reach.
Must it be—one to teach?
Follow the path with the most heart
And always reach for a new start.
Each day of life, live as the last
Reach to the infinite, make it your path.

Family

You brought her home today.
A bundle of joy for which you'd prayed.
Her care you've placed above your own.
Your house is now a families' home.
She's changed you more than words can say.
For her well-being you daily pray.
She has changed the path you've taken
Other roads are now forsaken.
She'll share with you her path of light
Thru her you'll see a different right
The parent's role is one of wonder
Love, amazement gentle and tender.
You've earned this very special place
You've blessed by His holy grace.

A FEW MORE POEMS

People

The spark of life that shapes us all,
Sets within us a special call.
Some to do great works of art,
Some will learn from taking things apart.
Some are great teachers,
Others are great speaker
Some know how to make money.
Others know how to make a day sunny
Some are farmers who work with the soil.
Other are laborers who live through toil.
Whatever the call
Wherever the start.
I know you'll be special.
I know it in my heart.

Birthday Celebration

Seasons come and seasons go.
Into each heart God does bestow.
Knowledge of life's ups and downs.
And sometimes a little piece of ground,
To nurture, tend and grow some seeds
And fulfill life's inner needs,
To be a part of this grand scheme
And keep alive a precious dream...
Through the years, a voice is heard
That changes life with a few words.
Another year to celebrate
With a fancy birthday cake.
For many more birthdays we do pray.
May health and wealth forever stay.

A Schizophrenic Patient

Alone within herself
A frail, bit of a woman
Tormented—fear stares from frozen eyes,
To pierce the heart.
The face—transformed by pain
From a barren place.
Comes the voice—I will die.
Shattered schemes
Unattended dreams
Fear of life.
Fear of death.
A stranger to herself.

Later Love

For passion I lingered in a fear
Never daring to shed a tear.
Till a moment of truth set me free
And I realized what was to be.
Love with a man eluded me then.
But left me something to call kin,
The struggles we shared—she and I
Somehow, we managed to get by.
Her growth I watched with loving care
We never had much money to spare.
Support from my family I held dear.
It strengthened me through many a year.
My youth I spent in struggle and pain
Always praying I would gain
A love to help me through time.
Someone I could call mine.
This blessing came from out of the blue
And from that moment on I knew what to do
Love for the young is challenged by passion
Love when you're older isn't always in fashion.
Young folks think it's cold and unfeeling.
He and I know it tender and pleasing.
God has given us some time to spend together
And we'll cherish each moment forever.
Grant us some time to be cared for and loved.
May we never forget Thy blessings from above.
(Written for a friend when she finally found him!)

Saying Goodbye

If all things are for a purpose
What is the meaning then?
When folks come briefly into our lives
And then they're off again.
Friends bring so much to help us grow
As we travel this path of life.
They challenge us and interest us
And offer encouragement through the strife,
If Shakespeare's statement "To thyself be true"
Is meant for all mankind to heed
Then each must seek his chosen path
And relentlessly pursue his need,
To succeed and make his mark in space and time.
To understand and find his destiny
To discover who he is and what he is
And be blessed through all eternity.
We share our dreams and goals
And use our knowledge and skills
And find fulfillment and abundance
And live life fully with all its thrills.
We wish you success in all you do
And know we wish you wellness, too.
You know we hate to see you go
For things won't be the same you know!
Walk gently and with courage.
See the beauty along each mile,
Remember to love and that you are loved.
Never, ever forget to smile.
Be true to yourself.

The White Lady

Cocaine

The white lady sings a passionate song
As she lures the lover to embrace.
He never knows the path is wrong.
For he's entranced and held in place.
She whirls and dances in his head
As he soars to ecstasy.
She may leave him there for dead.
Or weave a web of fantasy.
For once she leads him down her path
His soul is hers to twist.
He will not rest 'til the fire is past.
And the white lady gives her bliss,
What tempts the soul to seek to risk?
What motivates the spirit to test?
Does some emptiness need to be filled?
What makes the White Lady such a thrill?
When you know the pleasure she does bring
Will you ever again be sane.
The lover that you cannot keep
Can you turn away and let her sleep?
Leave her there in your dreams.
Listen not to her screams.
It's you she'll trap if she can.
And you'll listen to each command.
The White Lady sings a troubled song.
Leave her now—you don't belong.